Treasurt

A classic story by Robert Louis Stevenson

Adapted by Gill Munton

Series Editor: Louis Fidge

Macmillan Education
Between Towns Road, Oxford OX4 3PP
A division of Macmillan Publishers Limited
Companies and representatives throughout the world

ISBN 1-4050-6028-X
ISBN-13 978-1-4050-6028-8

Text © Gill Munton, 2007
Design and illustration © Macmillan Publishers Limited, 2007

First published 2007

Design and layout by Anthony Godber
Illustrated by Ian Heard
Cover design by Linda Reed & Associates
Cover illustration by Ian Heard

The authors and publishers would like to thank the
following for permission to reproduce their material:
Jennifer Tweedie 'Ocean Travel' copyright © Jennifer Tweedie
1992 first published in *Another Very First Poetry Book* by
John Foster (Oxford University Press, 1992), reprinted by
permission of the author.

The authors and publishers would like to thank the following
for permission to reproduce their photographic material:
Alamy/Classic Image p96

Printed and bound in Egypt by Sahara Printing Company

2011 2010 2009 2008 2007
10 9 8 7 6 5 4 3 2 1

Contents

The main characters

Long John Silver
pirate leader and ship's cook

Ben Gunn
ex-pirate

Billy Bones
pirate

Blind Pew
beggar and ex-pirate

Jim Hawkins
adventurer

Captain Smollett
ship's captain

Squire Trelawney
respectable local man

Dr Livesey
respectable local man

The voyage of the Hispaniola

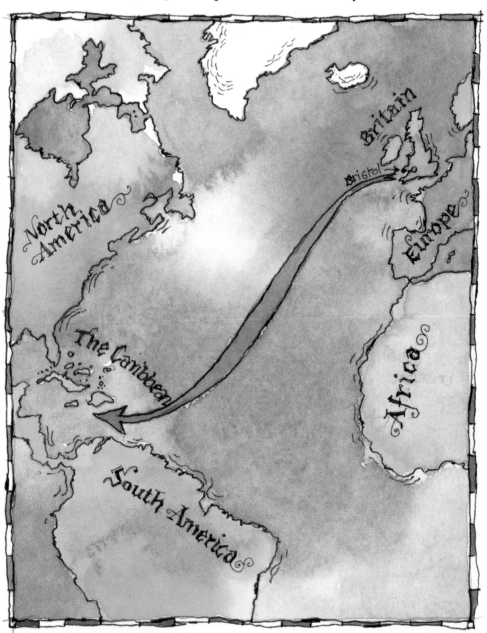

CHAPTER 1

Billy Bones and Blind Pew

My name is Jim Hawkins. When I was a boy, my mother and father had a guest house called the Admiral Benbow. And that is where my story begins.

I remember the pirate Billy Bones very well. He came walking up the road from the harbour: a big brown-skinned man in a dirty blue coat. He had long black hair and a scar across his cheek. Behind Billy another man pulled his sea chest along on a cart. I knew what it was because all sailors and pirates kept their belongings in sea chests. Billy Bones knocked on the door of our guest house with his stick.

When my father appeared, Billy said, 'I want a room.'

He threw four gold coins on the ground in front of my father. Then he turned to the man with the cart.

'Bring in my chest,' cried Billy.

I helped the man to carry the great sea chest up to the spare bedroom. It was so heavy that we were both glad to put it down. Billy Bones walked in afterwards and looked around the room. He smiled to himself and I decided that he must like the room.

Billy Bones stayed at the Admiral Benbow for weeks. Every day he climbed up onto the cliff and looked at the sea through a brass telescope. He spent the evenings in the guest house by the fire where he sang his old songs of the sea. He told stories of shipwrecks in terrible storms and men having exciting adventures.

If another sailor came to stay at the guest house, Billy peered at him and frowned.

One day he said to me, 'I'm hiding from a one-legged man. He wants to steal my sea chest, Jim. You must watch out for him and tell me if you see him.'

My father became ill during that time. Slowly he grew worse until one dark winter's day he finally died. My mother and I missed him terribly.

One foggy afternoon as I stood at the door of the Admiral Benbow thinking of my father, I saw a man slowly walking along the road. His eyes were covered and he wore a great cloak with a hood. He tapped the ground in front of him with a stick. As the man approached the guest house, he heard me moving by the door. He stopped in front of me.

'I am Blind Pew,' said the man. 'A poor, blind beggar. I became blind when I was fighting with a pirate. Will you please tell me where I am?'

'You are at the Admiral Benbow in Black Hill Cove,'
I told him.

'I hear a young voice. Will you lead me in?' he asked.

I held out my hand and Blind Pew pulled me towards
him.

'Take me to Billy Bones, boy,' he hissed, 'or I will break
your arm.'

Inside the guest house, Billy looked up and stared at
Blind Pew. He looked sick with fear.

'Hold out your hand, Billy,' ordered Pew. He pressed
a piece of paper into Billy's hand, and then disappeared.

I heard his stick tap-tapping down the road.

Billy staggered and put his hand to his throat.

'Pew has given me the black spot. He has killed me with
his curse,' he whispered.

And he fell to the floor, dead.

I told my mother what had happened. Without my father to look after us, we were both very frightened. There was a dead man in the guest house and a dangerous man not far away.

We ran to the village to get help. We went from house to house and begged each of the men to come back to the guest house with us. But no one dared to do it.

'You men have the courage of chickens,' my mother cried. 'My brave boy Jim and I will go back and face the danger alone. I will open that sea chest and take the money that Billy Bones owes us.'

We ran back to the guest house. It was foggy, but a full moon glowed red in the sky. We were afraid that someone might see us. My heart beat fast as we stepped through the door and locked it behind us.

My mother lit a candle. We went into the room where Billy Bones lay. He was just as we had left him: on his back with his eyes open and one arm stretched out. We pulled down the blinds so no one could see in.

Then my mother said, 'We need the key to the chest, Jim. It must be in one of his pockets. But I don't want to touch him.'

'I'll do it,' I offered.

I knelt down beside the body. There was a small circle of black paper near Billy's hand: the black spot. I picked it up and looked at it. Then I felt in his pockets. There were a few coins, a knife, a needle and thread and a compass. Nothing more.

'It may be around his neck,' said my mother.

I tore Billy's shirt open and found the key hanging on a bit of dirty string around his neck. I cut it off with his knife. Then we hurried upstairs with it to Billy's little room.

Inside the room we found the sea chest. It was still under the window where the man and I had left it. Billy had not moved it. The chest was old and battered. It had a letter 'B' on the lid.

'Give me the key,' said my mother.

I handed her the key and she put it in the lock. It was stiff, but after some struggling my mother opened it. She lifted the lid and we smelled tobacco and tar. On top there was a new suit, clean and folded. Under the suit we found a tin mug, a pair of guns, a Spanish watch, a few shells, but no money.

An old cloak lay at the bottom of the chest. My mother lifted it up impatiently. Inside the pocket she found a small packet tied up with string and a bag of gold coins.

'I'm an honest woman,' said my mother. 'I'll only take the money that he owes us.'

As she separated the British coins from the foreign ones, I heard a sound that almost made my heart jump into my mouth.

Outside the guest house, a stick was tap-tapping on the icy road. It was coming nearer and nearer. It tapped on the guest house door. Then the door handle turned and the lock rattled. We stood by the chest, hardly daring to breathe.

At last, there was silence. Then the stick tap-tapped away down the road and was gone.

'That was Blind Pew coming back for the gold coins,' I whispered to my mother. 'If the door hadn't been locked, he would have found us here. I know he will come back. Let's take the money you have counted and go.'

My mother jumped to her feet.

'I'll take this, too,' I said.

I picked up the little packet and put it in my pocket.

We hurried down the stairs and out of the guest house. The moon was shining brightly. Straight away we heard footsteps running towards us.

'Under the bridge. Quick!' I whispered, pointing to the little bridge outside the guest house.

I grabbed my mother's hand and pulled her under the bridge. We hid there in the long grass, trying to get our breath back.

From our hiding place, I peered out. Eight men stopped by the guest house door. One man held a lantern to light the way. I could see from the light that the men had black hair and ragged clothes. They looked like pirates. When I heard the high, shaky voice of Blind Pew, I knew I was right.

'In, in, in. And be quick,' he cried.

Five pirates got ready to break down the guest house door. Then one changed his mind and stopped. He turned the door handle and went in. We had left the door unlocked in our haste to get away. He was followed quickly by the other four pirates who ran inside to find Billy Bones' sea chest.

Meanwhile, Blind Pew waited outside with two men.

A cry of surprise came from inside the guest house followed by, 'Billy's dead.'

They had found Billy's body in the back room.

'Search him,' shouted Blind Pew. 'The rest of you can look for his sea chest.'

Feet pounded up the stairs and then there was silence. Suddenly Billy's bedroom window was opened. A man leaned out and shouted down to Blind Pew.

'Someone's been here already,' he explained.

'Is it there?' asked Pew.

'The money's here, if that's what you mean,' the voice answered.

'I don't care about the money. What about the packet?' asked Pew.

'It's gone, Pew,' came the reply.

'Those people from the guest house have taken it. They were here a few minutes ago – the door was locked then. Find them. They won't be far away,' shouted Blind Pew.

We heard the men looking in all the rooms of the Admiral Benbow. They went up and down the stairs so many times I thought they might break. My mother and I huddled together under the bridge.

After a few minutes, the pirates came out.

'They're not here,' cried one.

'We've looked everywhere,' said another.

Then we heard a whistle. It came from high on the hill behind the village. The pirates looked at each other in fear.

'The customs men are after us,' shouted one of the pirates. 'Let's run.'

'You cowards,' cried Pew. 'I'm not leaving without that packet. Oh, I wish I wasn't blind. I was the only one who dared to face Billy Bones. A blind man. And now you won't help me.'

'We've got the money, Pew. And the people from the guest house might have got the packet. We may never find it,' said the pirate.

Blind Pew was mad with anger. He raised his stick and beat the men around the back and shoulders. They put their arms up to protect themselves from the blows. Then I heard the sound of horses galloping. It came from the hill. Next came a gunshot.

When they heard the sound of gunfire, the pirates turned and ran. They left Blind Pew standing outside the guest house, tapping at the road with his stick.

'Don't leave me. Don't leave poor old Pew,' he cried.

In the moonlight, five men on horseback came galloping down the hill and into the road. Blind Pew screamed and ran. He fell into a ditch, but he jumped up again. He ran straight into one of the horses.

My mother fainted. I called out to the customs men. They helped me carry her into the guest house. Most of the furniture was broken, but nothing was missing except for the bag of coins.

'The other pirates have escaped, but we have got Pew,' said the man in charge. (I knew him. His name was Mr Dance.) 'What did they want, young Jim? More money?'

'I don't think so. I think they wanted something that is now in my pocket. I need to put it somewhere safe and to ask Dr Livesey for his advice,' I replied.

'Dr Livesey? He's a fine gentleman. He will advise you well,' said Mr Dance. He turned to one of his men. 'You have a strong horse,' he said. 'Take young Jim to Dr Livesey's house. And I'll come, too. I want to tell the doctor what happened.'

CHAPTER 2

The Hispaniola

When we arrived at Dr Livesey's house, Mr Dance told me to jump off the horse and knock on the door. I did as I was told and a maid came out. She told us that the doctor was visiting his friend Squire Trelawney.

We rode on to the Hall where Squire Trelawney lived. Another maid took me and Mr Dance to the squire's library. Here we found Squire Trelawney and Dr Livesey sitting by the fire. The doctor was smoking a pipe. He was a small man with a white wig and sharp, bright eyes.

Squire Trelawney was tall and red-faced with thick black eyebrows.

'Good evening, Dance,' the squire said warmly. 'And good evening to you, young Jim. What can we do for you?'

Mr Dance told the two men how Blind Pew and the pirates had broken into the Admiral Benbow and searched the place from top to bottom.

When he came to the part about the little packet, Doctor Livesey became very interested.

'Have you brought it with you, Jim?' he asked.

'Here it is, sir,' I replied and held it out to him.

Doctor Livesey looked at it and put it on the table.

'Now I must go,' explained Mr Dance. 'I still have work to do.'

After Mr Dance left the room, Squire Trelawney said, 'Stay for a while and have some cold pie.'

I was very hungry so I had a large piece of pie. Squire Trelawney and Dr Livesey talked while I ate it. I listened to them with interest.

'Trelawney, have you heard of Captain Flint?' asked Dr Livesey.

'I certainly have,' cried the squire. 'He was the cruellest pirate in the world.'

'Well, I have heard that Captain Flint robbed some ships. He stole their treasure and buried it,' explained Dr Livesey. 'No one knows where. But I have heard that Billy Bones was with Captain Flint when he buried the treasure. He may have helped him, too.

I also heard that Blind Pew and his men were looking for something in Billy's room this evening.

Now if Jim will allow us, we will open the packet and see what more it can tell us. Perhaps it will show us where to find this treasure.'

The doctor looked thoughtfully at the little packet on the table.

'Yes, open the packet,' I agreed.

I was very excited.

Doctor Livesey took out a pair of scissors. Carefully, he cut open the packet. Inside he found a book and a map. He opened the book and read a few pages.

'What does it say?' asked the squire.

'It tells me the names of the ships that Captain Flint robbed and sank,' he explained. 'It also tells me how much money Captain Flint paid Billy Bones to help him bury the treasure and to look after this map.'

Doctor Livesey unfolded the map and we all looked at it. It showed a small island that was about 15 kilometres long and eight kilometres across. There were some notes about how to find the island and where a ship could anchor. In the south-west part of the island, someone had marked a star in red ink. Underneath the star was a note saying: 'Treasure buried here.'

'Let's go to Bristol and hire a ship,' cried the squire. 'Let's go and find the treasure. We can have a ship ready in three weeks. I will be the admiral. Livesey, you will be ship's doctor and Jim, you will be the cabin boy. All we need is a captain and crew.'

'I will agree to do it,' said Dr Livesey. 'But I'm afraid of one man.'

'Who?' asked Squire Trelawney.

'You, Trelawney,' he replied. 'You talk too much. This is a secret we have to keep. There are plenty of wicked pirates out there who want that treasure and would be willing to do anything to get it. If any of them find out what we have, they will happily kill us all. We must talk to no one about this. Take two of your best men and go to Bristol, Trelawney. Find us a ship and a crew. Jim and I will join you as soon as we can.'

Before we could set off on our adventure, Doctor Livesey went to London on business. I stayed at the Hall. Redruth (the squire's servant) looked after me. I told no one about the map, but I felt very excited. I often explored the island in my mind. I imagined the men and the wild animals we might have to fight.

One day, a letter came for Dr Livesey. It was from the Old Anchor Guest House in Bristol. On the front it said, 'To be opened by Jim Hawkins if Dr Livesey is away.'

This is what I read:

 OLD ANCHOR, BRISTOL

1st March 1788

Dear Livesey

The ship is ready. She is called the Hispaniola and the workmen have prepared her well.

It was difficult to find a good honest crew. So many Bristol men are pirates. Then quite by chance I met a man on the dock called Long John Silver. He knows all the sailors in Bristol. It didn't take him long to find the rest of our crew.

Soon we will be hunting treasure. Join me as soon as you can. Tell young Jim to spend a night at the Admiral Benbow to say goodbye to his mother. But Redruth my servant must go with him.

Yours

John Trelawney

I was pleased with the letter. But I had one worry. What if Long John Silver was the one-legged pirate that Billy Bones was so afraid of?

When I arrived at the Admiral Benbow, it felt strange. Since I had last been there, quite a few things had changed. It did not look like the home I'd left in such a hurry. Squire Trelawney had repaired the broken furniture and had even added some new pieces. He had paid for the guest house to be repainted, too.

My mother was well. She was happy to see me and very happy with the repairs the squire had made to our home. She showed me the repaired furniture first and then the new furniture.

'What a kind man Squire Trelawney is,' she said to me.

After dinner the next day, I said goodbye to my mother. Then Redruth and I left my old home and set off for Bristol. One of my last thoughts was of Billy Bones, walking along the cliff top with his brass telescope.

We travelled all night. When our carriage arrived at Bristol, we walked through the docks to the guest house where Squire Trelawney was staying. I was delighted with all the tall ships and the sailors who sang as they mended sails or climbed the ropes. Soon I would be off to sea myself to search for buried treasure.

Squire Trelawney met us with a wide smile.

'Dr Livesey arrived last night,' he said. 'So everyone is here.'

'When do we sail, sir?' I asked him.

'Tomorrow,' he replied.

In the morning, Squire Trelawney gave me a note addressed to Long John Silver at the Spyglass Guest House.

'You'll find it quite easily,' he told me. 'Walk through the docks until you see a guest house sign with a telescope painted on it.'

Long John Silver was a tall strong man with a smiling face. Although he only had one leg, he moved easily with the help of a crutch. I stopped worrying. This friendly man could not possibly be a pirate.

I walked up to him and gave him the note.

'Mr Silver, sir?' I asked.

'Yes, my lad. And who are you?' he asked. He took the note and read it. 'Ah! You are our cabin boy.'

He shook my hand.

Next, I went to meet Squire Trelawney and Dr Livesey. They were going to inspect the *Hispaniola*.

We found the *Hispaniola* in the docks and eagerly climbed on board. A sailor met us and turned to Squire Trelawney.

'The captain wants to speak to you, sir,' he said.

'Take us to him,' the squire replied.

Captain Smollett was a cross-looking man who did not appear to be pleased to meet us. He shook our hands quickly with little warmth.

'Are we ready to go to sea?' asked the squire.

'I don't like the crew,' the captain replied.

At this answer, Dr Livesey was rather surprised. He looked first at Squire Trelawney, then at me and finally at the captain.

'Captain Smollett, tell us why you don't like the men,' he said.

'They think they know more than I do about sailing a ship. They're putting everything in the wrong place. And they talk too much. Even Long John Silver's parrot knows that we are going to hunt for treasure,' he replied.

'His parrot?' asked Dr Livesey.

'He has a large green parrot that sits on his shoulder,' explained the captain.

'I see,' said Dr Livesey. 'Now, what do you want to do about it?'

'I want to choose my own crew,' replied the captain. 'These men talk too much. I've heard them whispering. I'll tell you a secret, shall I? You have a map of an island. There is a red star on it to show you where the treasure lies. And there are instructions telling you how to find the island. All the men know about it.'

'But I told no one,' cried Squire Trelawney.

'We must take care,' continued Captain Smollett. 'No one must see the map. Let's lock our guns and gunpowder safely away from the men.'

'Don't you trust them?' asked Dr Livesey.

'No, I don't,' he answered. 'If you want me to be your captain, you must take my advice.'

'Very well,' agreed Dr Livesey. 'No one will see the map. And we will lock up the guns.'

Captain Smollett left the room and went onto the deck to collect the guns. We followed him.

As we were moving the guns and the gunpowder, Long John Silver climbed up the side of the ship.

'What are you doing?' he asked.

'We're moving the guns,' answered Captain Smollett.

'But we'll miss the tide,' complained Silver.

'That's not your business, Silver. You are only the cook. Now go and make dinner for the men,' ordered the captain.

Silver disappeared into the galley.

CHAPTER 3

Pirates!

When the ship was ready, Captain Smollett ordered the crew to pull up the anchor. As the big white sails filled with wind, the *Hispaniola* set off for Treasure Island.

It was a long journey. At the beginning, the sailors worked well. They all liked Long John Silver. He gave them plenty of food and he kept a barrel of apples on the deck for them. He was kind to me, too. He always seemed pleased to see me whenever I went into the galley. He kept it very clean and tidy.

A large green parrot sat in a cage in the galley.

'The parrot's name is Captain Flint,' Silver told me. 'I named him after the famous pirate. He wishes us luck, don't you, Captain Flint?'

'Pieces of eight, pieces of eight,' cried the parrot.

I knew that pieces of eight were gold coins.

'He's two hundred years old and he's been all around the world,' said Silver.

He pushed a piece of sugar through the bars of the cage.

Captain Smollet remained as unfriendly as the first day we met him. He spoke only when he was spoken to. He did not like Squire Trelawney so he tried not to speak to him at all. But he was pleased with his ship and his hard-working crew.

One day, Captain Smollett called out, 'We're nearly there, lads. We should reach Treasure Island tonight.'

This put everyone in a good mood and all the men worked harder. They sang as they worked and the ship sailed through the water at a great pace.

That night, I was on my way to my bed when I felt quite hungry. I wanted something to eat.

I'll go up on deck and take an apple from the barrel, I said to myself.

It was quite dark on deck. The only sounds I heard were the swish of the sea and the whistling of the man who was the ship's lookout. He was in the crow's nest looking for the island.

I looked inside the barrel. It was almost empty and I had to climb in to reach an apple. I was very tired after my day's work and I fell asleep inside the barrel.

I woke when I heard a man's voice. It was Long John Silver. When I had heard him speak a few words, I knew that I had to stay in the barrel and listen.

This is what I heard.

'Flint was our captain. His ship was called the *Walrus*. I lost my leg on that journey and Pew lost his eyes. But all the other pirates were afraid of me – and so was Flint,' explained Silver.

'But where are all those pirates now? Pew is a prisoner, but what about the others?' asked a younger man.

'Perhaps some of them are on this ship,' laughed Silver. He continued, 'A pirate's life is a hard life. But you can make a lot of money. If you keep your money safe, you can live like a king. My wife looks after my money – that's how I keep it safe.'

'I'll help you get the treasure,' said the younger man.

I sat quite still in the barrel. So Long John Silver *was* a pirate and he wanted to steal the treasure. And this young man wanted to help him. But what about the others?

Then a third voice joined in.

'Nearly all the men are on your side, Silver. But how long must we pretend to be honest sailors? When can we become pirates?' the voice asked.

'Not yet,' replied Silver. 'We need Captain Smollett to sail the ship. I haven't seen the map so I don't know where to find the treasure. I have a plan, though. We will wait until Livesey and Trelawney dig it up and load it on the ship. Then we will strike.'

'What will we do with Dr Livesey and the others?' asked the younger man.

'We'll kill them, of course,' answered Silver. 'Now, get me an apple, lad. I'm feeling hungry.'

I froze. They would find me now. What could I do? Run? But where to?

But then the third man said, 'We can do better than apples, Silver. Let's go down to your galley and see what we can find.'

Before Silver could reply, the lookout cried out.

'Land ahoy!' he shouted.

We had reached Treasure Island.

Everyone came running up from the cabins and onto the deck. I jumped out of the barrel and followed the pirates to the bow of the ship. We all looked towards the island. I could see three hills, one with its peak hidden by mist.

Captain Smollett ordered the crew to take down the biggest sail.

Then he said, 'Has anyone been on this island before?'

'I have, sir,' said Silver. 'I once stopped here for water.'

'I think we can anchor to the south of the island. Is that right, Silver?' asked the captain. 'Look at this map. Here's the place.'

I watched Silver as he took the map and looked at it in the moonlight. But it wasn't the map I had found in Billy Bones' chest. Someone had copied it. And, of course, they had left out the red star.

Silver said, 'That's right, sir.'

He turned to me and for a moment I was terrified. But of course, he didn't know I had been hiding in the apple barrel when he had been talking to the pirates. He didn't know I had heard everything and knew of his plans.

'It's a fine island for a boy,' said Silver. He put his hand on my shoulder. 'You can swim and climb trees and run about. Tell me when you want to explore and I'll make you a picnic.'

Then he went down to the galley.

Silver was gone. Now I had a chance to tell Dr Livesey and Squire Trelawney what I had heard. But they were talking to the captain and I didn't want to interrupt. Then Dr Livesey came over to me and asked me to fetch his pipe from his cabin. This was my chance. I took it.

'Dr Livesey, I have some terrible news. Take the squire and the captain down to your cabin. Send for me so I can tell you all in private,' I said.

Dr Livesey frowned, but he did as I asked.

Inside the doctor's cabin I found the doctor, the squire and the captain sitting around a table. As I walked through the door, they looked up at me with concern.

'Now, Jim,' said the squire. 'You have something to tell us. What is it?'

I told them everything I had heard in the apple barrel. They listened carefully and no one interrupted me.

When I had finished, Dr Livesey said, 'Thank you, Jim. It's a good thing you found out. And you have been very brave to tell us. I am sure you were very afraid.'

Squire Trelawney turned to Captain Smollett.

'I'm sorry, Captain. You were right about the crew and I was wrong,' he said. 'They *are* a band of cruel pirates.'

'Those pirates kept their deadly secret very well. It was easy to be fooled by them,' answered the captain. 'Now, I'll tell you what we should do. Number one. We can't turn back. If we do, they will attack us at once. So we must keep going. Number two. If we keep going, they won't attack us until we have found the treasure. They don't know where it is so they need to wait until we have found it. Number three. Some of the men are still on our side. We must keep them on our side. Then we should attack when the pirates don't expect it. We must take them by surprise.'

'I agree, Captain,' said Dr Livesey. 'And, in the meantime, Jim can help us to keep control. The men trust him and he notices everything.'

We counted up the men who were on our side. There were seven men including me, but I was only a boy. There were many more pirates against us. It would not be a fair fight when it came.

I left the doctor's cabin and went on deck. I saw that the *Hispaniola* was a little less than one kilometre south-east of the island. It was a sunny day without a cloud in the sky.

From the deck, I could see pine forests on the island. Waves roared and crashed on the sandy beaches that lined the island. It was more magical than I had imagined. Although I had dreamed of visiting the island night after night, I no longer looked forward to exploring it. I knew that soon we would have to fight the pirates. I was afraid and they outnumbered us. Would we win the fight? I was not sure.

There was no wind so the ship could not move any closer to the island. We dropped anchor and got the rowing boats ready.

It was at this time that the crew became lazy and rude. But Long John Silver did not. Instead, he obeyed all his orders. He smiled and sang as he worked.

'He wants to keep everybody happy until it's time to fight,' whispered Captain Smollett. 'I think we'll let some of the men go ashore to cheer them up.'

The captain decided to keep six of the crew aboard the *Hispaniola* and let the others go ashore.

Captain Smollett asked Long John Silver to organise the men. They cheered when they heard the news. Seagulls fluttered in the sky and squawked at the noise.

I jumped into one of the rowing boats unseen and hid under a sail. The two boats raced for the shore. My boat arrived at the beach first.

I leaped out of the boat onto the shore without being seen by the other sailors. I ran and ran until I could run no further. Soon, I was in a thick forest where I found strange and beautiful plants. I even saw some snakes.

Suddenly, a flock of wild ducks flew up from a little river. They screamed and circled in the air. Some of the men must have been nearby. I hid among the trees. I heard voices, but I was too far away to hear what they were saying. Slowly, I crawled closer. I peered through the leaves and saw Silver talking to one of the sailors.

'If you are not on my side, Tom, I will have to kill you,' I heard him say. 'I want that treasure and I will do anything to get it.'

'I'm an honest sailor,' replied the man. 'Captain Smollett is my captain, not you.'

The man turned and walked back towards the beach. With a fierce cry, Long John Silver leaped on the man and killed him with his knife.

Everything seemed to spin round and round. I almost fainted. Then Silver pulled out a whistle and blew it several times. He was calling his men. I crept back the way I had come and ran for my life.

CHAPTER 4

Ben Gunn to the rescue

A head of me, a large rock came loose and rolled down the hillside. Someone was up there watching me. I stopped and looked up. A man leaped behind a tree.

Was it one of the pirates? Silver was behind me and this man was in front of me. I was trapped and I was tired. I started to run back the way I came.

As I ran, I looked back over my shoulder. The man reappeared and started to run. He was moving as fast as a deer. Then I remembered my gun and reached for it. When he saw what I was doing, the man stopped running and took a step towards me.

At last we met. He knelt down in front of me and held out his hands.

'Don't shoot me,' he begged. His voice was creaky like a rusty lock.

'Who are you?' I asked.

'My name is Ben Gunn,' he replied. 'I haven't spoken to another human being for three years.'

His skin was sunburned and his clothes were rags. When I looked more closely, I saw that they were made of old bits of sail held together with rope.

'Three years?' I asked. 'What happened to you? Were you in a shipwreck?'

'No. I used to be a pirate, but I argued with my captain and he left me on this island. I eat berries and fish from the sea. But I dream about … cheese.'

'You will have all the cheese you can eat if you help me,' I told him.

He looked at me.

'What's your name?' he asked.

'Jim,' I replied.

'Well, Jim, perhaps you can help me to get away from this island. And perhaps I can help you. I'm a rich man,' said Ben Gunn.

I thought he was crazy. How could such a man be rich?

'I know you came here on that ship, Jim. Is it Flint's ship?' he asked.

This idea seemed to terrify him.

'No, it isn't Flint's ship. Flint is dead. But some of his pirates are on board. When we set sail for the island, we didn't know that most of our crew were pirates,' I explained.

'Is there a man with one leg? Tell me he's not there,' Ben Gunn cried.

He grabbed my arm and held it tightly.

'Are you talking about Silver?' I asked.

'Yes, that was his name,' he replied.

'He's the ship's cook and the leader of the pirates,'
I explained.

Then I told this strange man the whole story. Somehow,
I knew that I could trust him.

When I had finished, Ben said, 'Well, you and your
friends are in trouble, that's for sure. But you're a good
lad, Jim, I can see that. If I help you to find the treasure
and get rid of the pirates, will Squire Trelawney pay me?
Will he share the treasure with me and give me a ride
home on his ship? I'm a good sailor and you'll need help
to sail her when the pirates are gone.'

'I'm sure Squire Trelawney will agree to that,' I said.
'He's a fair man and we need all the help we can get.'

Ben gave a sigh of relief.

'Now I will tell you my story,' he said. 'I was on Flint's
ship when he brought the treasure to this island. When
his crew had buried it, he killed everyone except Silver,
Pew, Billy Bones and me. We had stayed on the ship. And
then we set sail for home.

Three years ago I came to the island on another ship.
We searched for the treasure for twelve days. We couldn't
find it and the captain was angry.

On the twelfth day he gave me a shovel and said,
"You can stay here and find Flint's treasure by yourself."
Then he sailed away and left me on my own. I've been
here since that day.'

Then he thought of something else.

'I've got a little boat, Jim,' he told me. 'It's hidden under the white rock. We may need it.'

Suddenly I heard the sound of a cannon.

'The pirates on the *Hispaniola* are firing the cannon. They've started fighting,' I cried. 'Come on, Ben.'

We ran back to the boats on the beach. Ben knew the island well and he showed me a quick way to get there.

We heard more cannon fire and gunshots. And then, above the trees ahead of me, I saw a flag fluttering in the breeze. It was the Union Flag, the flag of my country.

Dr Livesey continued the story in his diary.

My good friend Trelawney asked me if we should try to overpower the six pirates remaining on the ship and sail away. I told him that Captain Smollett had said there wasn't enough wind. Also, we thought that Jim had gone ashore and we couldn't leave him behind.

I was very worried about Jim. He was on the island with a band of dangerous men. We decided that I would go ashore with Hunter (one of Trelawney's men) to see what we could find out.

We left the six pirates on board. They grumbled, but they stayed on the ship. Then we rowed to the island.

I told Hunter that the map showed a wooden building not far from shore. Some sailors built it long ago and I thought it would make a good place for our headquarters.

We pulled the little boat up onto the beach and set off for the building. It was a house made of logs and it was big enough to hold about forty men. There was a strong wooden fence around it and there was a stream nearby: fresh water at last.

Suddenly we heard a terrible cry.

'It's Jim,' I thought. 'The fighting has started and they've killed him.'

Hunter and I ran to the boat and rowed back to the Hispaniola to fetch Squire Trelawney, Captain Smollett and the others. We loaded the rowing boat with meat, biscuits and guns. I took my medicine chest. Captain Smollett told the six pirates that if they signalled to anyone on the island, we would shoot them. There wasn't time to burn the other rowing boats.

We made several journeys. We knew Silver and his men were not far away. He had more men, but we had more guns. Then Captain Smollett persuaded one of the six pirates to join our side. We needed all the help we could get.

The last rowing boat was overloaded and there was a strong tide. It was hard to keep the little boat afloat and to steer it towards the landing place.

Suddenly, Captain Smollett cried out that we had forgotten the cannon. We looked behind us and saw the five pirates preparing to fire it. They fired the cannon and a cannonball flew past our heads. Trelawney took out his gun and fired back. One of the pirates fell to the deck. The other four screamed with rage and so did the pirates on the beach. They were all getting back into their rowing boats.

Our overloaded boat filled up with water. As we came close to the beach, it sank. We waded to the shore, angry because we had lost food and gunpowder in the water.

We ran as fast as we could to the wooden house. The pirates raced after us. As we arrived, seven pirates appeared before us and there was a fierce battle. The pirates lost one man and Redruth, Trelawney's servant, was shot. As the pirates retreated, we took him into the house, but sadly the poor man died. Trelawney was very upset.

Captain Smollett took the Union Flag from his pocket. He made a flagpole and tied the flag to it. Then he looked for food in our stores.

Captain Smollett asked me how long I thought we would be here. I told him it could be for months as we had to fight the pirates as well as find the treasure.

The captain told me there wasn't much food.

Then we heard a cannonball hit the side of the log house. And another.

Trelawney said the pirates couldn't see the log house from the Hispaniola, but they could see the flag. He suggested that we should take it down. But the captain refused. Then he said we could get food and gunpowder from the sunken rowing boat. But when we got near, we saw that we were too late. Silver and his men were picking up the supplies and rowing them back to the Hispaniola.

The captain sat down to write his log. I sat and worried about young Jim. Was he alive or dead? And then I heard a voice from behind the wooden fence. It was Jim. I ran to greet him as he climbed over the fence and joined us.

When Ben Gunn saw the Union Flag flying above the trees, he grabbed my arm.

'That's the British flag,' he said. 'Your friends are sheltering in Captain Flint's old log house.'

'What if it's the pirates?' I asked.

'No, pirates don't fly the Union Flag. Pirates always fly the Jolly Roger flag,' explained Ben Gunn.

'Let's go to the log house. You can meet Dr Livesey and Squire Trelawney,' I said.

'No, not yet,' replied Ben. 'I don't trust anyone. One of them must come and see me first. He'll find me where you first saw me. He must carry a white flag as a sign of peace.'

Then a cannonball flew through the trees and thudded into the sand. Ben ran into the wood and I set off for the log house.

More cannonballs fell and I ran from one hiding place to another. The cannonballs were aimed at the log house and I didn't dare go too near it.

Soon I was back on the beach. The tide was right out and I could see the *Hispaniola*. The cannon fire was over, but I noticed something that almost made my heart stop. The pirate flag – the Jolly Roger – was flying above the ship.

CHAPTER 5

The white flag

I decided that it was safe to go back to the log house. On the way, I saw a large white rock among some bushes near the beach. Was it the white rock where Ben Gunn's boat was hidden?

I kept walking and reached the log house at last. I climbed over the high fence and called out to Dr Livesey. He came to meet me.

'Jim,' he cried. 'Thank goodness, you're back. I'm so pleased to see you. We heard a scream and we thought the pirates had killed you.'

Dr Livesey took me into the log house where the others greeted me warmly.

'You're alive,' cried Squire Trelawney. 'Thank goodness for that.'

'Good to have you back with us, young Jim,' said Captain Smollet.

I looked around the house. Everything was made of rough logs: the walls, the roof and the floor. A cold wind blew sand through the gaps in the walls and soon we had sand in our hair, mouths and eyes. There was even sand in our kettle. There was a fireplace with a square hole in the roof for a chimney so we lit a fire.

Captain Smollett gave everyone a job to do. Two men went to collect wood for the fire. Dr Livesey was to be our cook and the rest of us guarded the log house.

I was on guard at the door when Dr Livesey came out for some fresh air. While we were alone, I told him about my earlier adventures on the island.

'I wanted to explore the island so I climbed into one of the boats and hid under a sail. When we reached the shore I jumped out and ran. No one saw me so I kept going until I found myself in the woods,' I told him. 'Then I heard Silver talking to one of the men. I hid in the trees to listen to what he was saying. I heard the man saying he wanted to be on our side. This made Silver so angry that he killed the man.'

Dr Livesey frowned.

'I ran away,' I went on. 'Then I saw a man on the hillside. He was hiding among the trees. I thought he was one of the pirates. I had my gun so I went towards him. I was shocked when we met. His skin was burned almost black by the sun and his clothes were rags.

His name is Ben Gunn. He told me he used to be a pirate, but he had an argument with his captain. He was left all alone on the island. He's been here for three years. He eats what he can find: berries and fish, but he dreams of cheese. He promised to help us if we will take him back to England on the *Hispaniola*.'

'I'm glad he is on our side,' Dr Livesey replied with a smile. 'But he may be a little mad if he has been on the island for three years without any human company. Did you say he liked cheese?'

'Yes, sir,' I replied.

'I have a piece in my pocket. I will keep it for Ben Gunn,' laughed the doctor.

After dinner that evening Captain Smollett spoke to us all. 'We don't have much food. We must defeat the pirates and take back our ship soon,' he said.

We discussed what we should do. Then finally Dr Livesey said that I should go to bed. I was very tired and I slept well that night.

In the morning, I was woken by Captain Smollett's surprised voice.

'Long John Silver's coming. And he's carrying a white flag,' he shouted.

I jumped out of bed and ran to the fence outside. I could see Silver through one of the gaps between the logs.

'Back inside, men,' cried the captain. 'It may be a trick.'

From behind the high wooden fence, Silver called out to the captain.

'I want to make peace,' he cried.

Silver threw his crutch over the fence and climbed after it. He limped towards Captain Smollett who was standing blocking the doorway.

'Won't you let me into the house?' he asked. 'I want to talk to you and it's a cold morning.'

Captain Smollett refused so Silver sat down on the sand by the door.

'What a pretty house,' he said. 'And there's Jim. Good morning, Jim. What a happy family you must be.'

'If you have something to say, say it now,' said the captain coldly.

He was not in the mood for playing games.

'Very well,' said Silver. 'We want that treasure. We know you have a map to show where it is buried. If you give me the map, we will spare your lives. Then I will give you a choice: you can come back to England with us on the *Hispaniola* or you can stay here. I'll send another ship to fetch you if you choose to stay.'

Captain Smollett stood up.

'Is that all you have to say?' he cried. His voice was angry. 'Now you listen to me, Silver. You are in no position to be giving me orders. One: you can't find the treasure without the map. Two: you can't sail the ship. Three: if you fight us you will lose. Now I will give *you* a choice: give yourselves up and I will take you back to England for a fair trial. Or you can fight us and we will win. Now go away and leave us in peace.'

Silver wasn't expecting this answer. He was angry.

'Help me over the fence, then,' he cried.

'I will not,' replied the captain.

Silver glared at him.

'Your log house will soon be a pile of sticks and you'll all be dead,' he cried.

Silver threw his crutch back over the fence in anger. Captain Smollett watched as he struggled over the fence and landed with a thud on the other side. He listened as Silver picked up his crutch and rapidly limped away through the trees.

When the captain was sure Silver had gone, he turned round and was surprised to find a small crowd behind him. All the guards had left their places to listen. Captain Smollett was angry and sent them all back to their places.

Then he said, 'You heard what I said to Silver. He will soon be back with his men so we must be ready for them.'

Then he went to check the guns and the knives.

The sun was shining now, so we took off our coats and rolled up our sleeves. We waited for Silver and his men to return with our weapons in our hands. I felt my heart pounding in my chest. It was a mixture of excitement and terrible fear that had set it pumping blood though my body fast enough for me to fight or run.

Suddenly we heard a shot. One of our men had fired his gun. Then the pirates attacked. They fired shot after shot at the log house from every side. Then there was silence.

A group of pirates ran out of the woods and climbed over the fence.

We fought fiercely in the log house and outside it. I was nearly killed when one of the pirates lifted his long knife above his head. I leaped out of the way, but my foot slipped in the soft sand and I rolled to the bottom of the hill.

In the end, six pirates and three of our men were killed. My hand was cut so Dr Livesey bandaged it for me. But that was nothing. Captain Smollett was badly hurt. He had a broken shoulder and a cut leg.

Luckily, the pirates did not come back so we rested. Squire Trelawney and I cooked some meat for dinner while the doctor looked after the injured men.

After dinner, Dr Livesey and the squire sat down next to Captain Smollett. He was lying on a rough wooden bed with his leg in a bandage. The three men talked for a long time. I tried to listen to what they were saying. But I only heard the words 'Ben Gunn' and 'wants to see one of us.'

After some time, Dr Livesey picked up his gun and his knife. Carefully, he folded the treasure map and put it in his pocket. He took a handkerchief for a white flag. He climbed over the fence and disappeared among the trees. I knew he was going to see Ben Gunn.

CHAPTER 6

Alone in a boat

It was very hot in the log house and there was no way to cool it down. I wished I was with Dr Livesey, walking in the cool shade of the pine trees.

As I cleared away the dinner things, thoughts raced through my mind. If Silver attacked again, what would happen? How would we keep our food supplies stocked if Silver was on the *Hispaniola*? What would happen when we ran out of gunpowder? Then, all of a sudden, I had an idea.

I made sure that no one was looking and filled my pocket with biscuits from the food store. I picked up my gun and left the house. I was going to return to the white rock and find Ben Gunn's little boat.

It was early evening when I set off, but the sun was still beating down. It was as hot outside the log house as it was inside it. I walked through the woods so the pirates would not see me. Even walking through the shady pine woods left me hot and thirsty.

When I came near to the beach, I heard the sound of waves crashing on the shore. There was a strong wind coming off the sea and at last I felt cooler.

I looked out at the sea. I could see the *Hispaniola* in the distance. Silver and another pirate were climbing off the ship and into a rowing boat. They were talking and laughing. They must be coming ashore.

I heard a distant scream. I felt afraid, but then I smiled. It was only Captain Flint the parrot.

Soon I saw the white rock ahead of me. It took me a long time to reach it because I had to crawl through thick bushes. When at last I reached the rock, a thick fog covered the island and it was almost dark.

I felt in the long grass below the white rock with my fingers. Nothing at first. And then my hand touched something soft and furry. I pushed back the grass and found a little tent made of goatskins. I opened the flap and peered inside. There, inside the goatskin tent, was a little rowing boat.

I looked at Ben Gunn's work. He had done a fine job. It was made of more pieces of goatskin that were stretched over a wooden frame. There were two oars inside it. I pulled the boat carefully out of its hiding place to get a better look at it. It was very small.

Too small for a man, I thought. *But just perfect for me.*

It was light and easy to carry. It would do the job
I had planned very well.

I will row out to the Hispaniola *and cut the anchor rope,*
I thought. *Then the ship will drift away, leaving Long John
Silver on the island.*

I sat down on the grass and waited for darkness. I ate a
few biscuits and thought about my plan. It was still very
foggy so there was no moonlight. If I was careful, no one
would see me.

As soon as it was dark, I stood up and looked around.
I saw some pirates sitting by a fire on the beach, singing
and shouting. In the distance a single yellow light shone
on the *Hispaniola*.

I carried the little boat down to the sea, put it in the
water and climbed in. Then I picked up the oars and
rowed hard. The sea was as black as the sky above.

As I rowed towards the *Hispaniola*, she looked like
a tall castle rising out of the sea. It was hard work rowing,
but luckily, the tide swept me towards her.

At last I reached the ship and found the anchor rope.
A cabin window was open and I could hear loud, angry
voices: two pirates were arguing.

There was a gust of wind and the *Hispaniola* moved
towards me. I cut the anchor rope with a quick slash of
my knife. But then the ship started spinning around and
I had to row with all my strength to get away from it.

Once I had steadied myself, I came alongside the ship
again. Then I stood up carefully in my boat and peered
through the open windows into the lighted cabin.

Inside the cabin I saw two angry, red-faced men. One man stood up from the table, knocking his chair over, and punched the other man. He fell to the floor, but quickly got up to return a punch. Soon the two pirates were rolling around the floor fighting fiercely. It was clear that no one had noticed that the ship was drifting slowly out to sea.

I sat down again in my little boat and waited. Suddenly, the *Hispaniola* turned. I heard running feet and more shouts: the pirates had noticed that something was wrong.

I was too tired to row back to the safety of the shore. Instead, I lay in the bottom of my little boat and hid. I hoped the men would not look overboard and see my little boat bobbing up and down in the water. As the waves rocked the boat gently, my mind filled with all the strange things that had happened to me. It had all started with the arrival of Billy Bones at our little guest house. This led me to think of the Admiral Benbow and my mother who was running the guest house without me. I thought of my dead father and my comfortable life before I set off on this dangerous journey. Soon, I was fast asleep.

When I woke up, the sea was very rough. I was thrown from side to side in my little boat. The sun was shining brightly, but there was a strong wind. I could see the shore in the distance so I took up the oars and rowed towards it. But it was no good. The sea was too rough. I lay back down in the boat to rest and wait. Somehow, the boat managed to stay afloat and not sink while it bounced up and down on the waves.

After a while, when the water was calmer, I sat up and looked for the shore. It was further away now. Again I picked up the oars and rowed towards it. But it was still too difficult. As I pulled on the oars, great waves poured into my boat. Soon I was soaked and shivering.

I looked for the shore, too tired to row any more. To my horror, I could no longer see it at all. I realised that the tide had dragged me further and further in the opposite direction. Rowing against the tide was impossible.

What will happen to me? I wondered in fear. *Will I ever get back to the island again?*

I was terribly thirsty, but I had nothing to drink. I found my lips were thick with salt when I licked them. This made my throat burn and made me feel worse. I shivered from the cold. I had been soaked by the waves that had poured over the boat. When the wind blew over my damp body, I shivered even more. I began to panic and I feared for my life.

Will I die a lonely death of thirst and cold in this tiny boat? I asked myself. *Will I ever be found?*

Thoughts like these soon tired me out so I lay back down in the boat to rest. As I waited for the wind to die down again, the little boat was thrown back and forth by the waves once more. I lay inside and clung to the sides of the boat. I was at the mercy of the sea. It could take me wherever it pleased and I could do nothing about it.

When I next looked out of my boat, I saw I was drifting towards the *Hispaniola*. The pirates had put her sails up and she was sailing north-west around the island.

Soon the ship changed direction and drifted towards me. This confused me. Why had the pirates turned away from the island?

Have they seen me? I asked myself.

No, they hadn't, for the ship changed direction again. I decided that the pirates must be having difficulty steering the ship.

'What terrible sailors those pirates are,' I said out loud.

When the ship changed direction again, I realised that no one was steering it.

If the pirates are not steering the ship, where are they? I wondered.

Perhaps I could get on board and sail the *Hispaniola* back to shore. Then I could return her to Captain Smollett. Everyone would be very pleased with me.

At that moment, a huge wave crashed over the little boat and filled it with water. My heart pumped wildly. I reached for my oars and rowed towards the ship with all my strength. More water filled the boat. I was afraid I would sink. I rowed as hard as I could.

After a while, I realised that the tide had turned and the wind had dropped. No longer was the sea taking me where it pleased. It had calmed and I was able to row towards the ship. With the help of the tide, my boat quickly reached the *Hispaniola*.

Soon I was close enough to see that the cabin window was still open. Inside, the table lamp was still burning in the daylight. No one had put it out. No one was on the deck, either. Where were the pirates?

Suddenly, my little boat rose to the top of a wave and I was level with the deck of the *Hispaniola*. This was my chance. I stood up and jumped. I grabbed a rope on the side of the ship and clung to it as the waves crashed against my body.

Eventually I found the strength to climb over the side of the ship and drag myself onto the deck. As I lay on the deck, I heard a crunching sound. My little boat had been crushed by the *Hispaniola*. It sank beneath the waves.

CHAPTER 7

Captain Jim

On board the *Hispaniola* I lay on the deck, out of breath. I *had* to get up before the pirates found me. I listened for their voices. But it was strangely silent. Only the sound of a broken bottle rolling back and forth could be heard. There were the dirty footprints of the pirates all over the unwashed deck. But there was no one in sight. Where were they?

Slowly, I stood up and walked along the deck. As the main sail moved, I caught sight of a pirate lying on his back. At once I could see that he was dead. I made my way towards him and caught sight of a second pirate. He was sitting with his back against the side of the ship. His chin rested on his chest, but I could still see his face clearly. I knew this man's name: it was Hands. His face was very white and he was very still.

Was he dead, too? I wondered.

No. Slowly, Hands turned his head towards me. He looked at me, but it was too much effort for him. His eyes rolled in his head.

'Water,' he groaned. 'Please give me water.'

I thought quickly. Hands looked very ill. He was too weak to fight me. And he might be useful.

'Don't worry, Hands,' I said. 'I'll find you some water in the galley.'

I ran down the stairs.

Down in the galley, I looked around in horror. I had never seen such a mess. All the cupboards had been left open and were covered in black handprints. There were broken plates and scraps of food everywhere. Like the deck, the floor was covered with dirty footprints and empty bottles rattled in the corners of the room. One of Dr Livesey's books was open on the table. Several pages had been torn out.

I found a bottle full of water and drank it all. I picked up another one for Hands. Then I looked in the open cupboards for food. It was a long time since I had eaten and that had only been some biscuits. I soon found some cheese and pickles. Quickly, I grabbed the food and ran up to the deck with it. I gave Hands the bottle of water and he drank it at once without stopping for breath.

As Hands drank his water, I sat down to eat my food alongside him. I was very hungry and the food made me feel much better. When I had eaten, I sat back and looked at Hands. He looked much better for drinking all that water. But he was still very pale.

'Are you badly hurt?' I asked him.

'I am,' he grunted. Then he pointed to the man on the deck. 'But he's dead.'

I looked at the dead man.

'What happened to him, Hands?' I asked.

'I'll tell you what happened,' he answered. 'He and I were left alone on the ship. We put the sails up. We were going to sail away. But then we had an argument and now he's dead.'

I shuddered.

'What are you doing here, Jim?' asked Hands.

'I've come to take over the ship,' I replied.

'Very well,' said Hands.

He did not have the strength to stop me.

'You can call me Captain. And there's another thing,' I said.

'Yes, Captain?' said Hands.

'I'm taking that Jolly Roger down,' I replied.

I pulled down the flag and threw it into the sea. Hands did nothing to stop me.

By now Hands was looking a little better.

'So you want to sail the ship to the beach and go ashore, do you, Jim?' he asked.

'Yes, I do,' I told him.

'I will help you, if you help me,' offered Hands. 'Give me food and drink and bandage my leg, and I will tell you how to sail the *Hispaniola*.'

'You may not be a good sailor, Hands. But you're a better sailor than I am,' I admitted.

We shook hands with each other to confirm the agreement, but we didn't trust each other. Would Hands keep his side of the deal? Immediately I put it to the test.

'Now help me take the ship to the beach near the log house,' I said. 'I don't want to take her back to the beach near Silver. I don't want to fight any more pirates.'

'I don't have a choice, do I? I will die without your help, Jim,' muttered Hands.

We set sail. The sun was shining and there was a strong wind. Soon the ship was sailing smoothly.

I had plenty to eat and drink and now I was captain of a ship. But Hands watched everything I did. He was waiting for me to make a mistake. I thought of the deal I had made with Hands. I had agreed to give him food and water and bandage his leg. He had kept his part of the deal so far, so I must do the same. I went to my cabin.

Inside the cabin, I opened my sea chest and took out an old silk handkerchief. I went back on deck with it and took it to Hands. Carefully, I bandaged the pirate's leg with it.

Soon we caught sight of Treasure Island. I breathed a sigh of relief. Only a few hours earlier I had feared I would never see the island again.

'Let's head for the island,' I said to Hands.

'Not so fast, Jim,' he replied. 'We can't sail against the tide. We will have to wait until it turns.'

I looked at Hands suspiciously. Was he telling the truth? I looked overboard at the racing water beneath us. But I could see he was right. I had already experienced the power of the tide in my little boat so I decided to do as Hands said.

We waited for the tide to turn so that we could sail the *Hispaniola* up to the beach by the log house.

Hands was still sitting with his back to the side of the ship. He stretched his bandaged leg out before him.

'Fetch me some more water, Jim,' he groaned. 'This warm weather has made me thirsty.'

I looked at his sly face. I didn't trust him. He couldn't be thirsty again already, could he?

He wants to get me out of the way, I thought. *But why?*

I soon found out.

When I went down the steps to the galley, I took off my boots. I crept through the cabins until I came to the bottom of the ladder in the bow of the ship. I climbed the ladder. Now I could see Hands, but he couldn't see me.

I watched him crawl across the deck on his hands and knees. I knew his leg hurt because he groaned as he moved. He stopped by a pile of ropes and pulled out something. It was a knife. He hid it in his jacket and crawled back to the side of the ship. He stretched out his bandaged leg again. Carefully, he got back into the same position as before so I wouldn't notice that he had moved.

Now that Hands had a weapon I was sure he would use it on me. He could fire the cannon to call all the other pirates, too. Then they could escape with the *Hispaniola*.

I was soon back on the deck with my boots on and another bottle of water in my hand. I passed the bottle to Hands and he drank it down. When he had drunk the water, he wiped his mouth.

'That feels better,' he said. 'But I'm still too weak to move.'

I knew this was not true. Hands had a knife inside his jacket and he would use it if he got the chance. I had to watch him very carefully.

Suddenly, Hands called out, 'Look, Jim, the tide has turned. We can sail the ship to the beach. Come on, I'll tell you how to do it.'

It was hard work steering the *Hispaniola*. For a while I forgot the danger I was in as I concentrated on steering the ship. But as we came up to the beach, I saw a shadow from the corner of my eye. I looked round and saw Hands coming towards me with the knife.

Our eyes met and he cried out in anger as he ran towards me. Quickly, I stepped aside and the blade missed me. It sank into the side of the ship. Hands pulled it out and went to attack me again. But this time I was ready for him. I grabbed hold of his arm and stopped another blow hitting me.

Back and forth we struggled until Hands managed to break free. Again he lashed out at me with his knife, but this time he cut my shoulder. I held it in pain, but was ready for the next blow. It didn't come. Hands was too badly hurt to fight any more. I took my chance and punched him with all the strength I had. He fell on the deck. It was all over.

Quickly, I tied Hands to the mast with some rope. Now I was safe. I could see him and he couldn't escape. I looked at my shoulder. It was still bleeding but the wound was not deep and it would heal soon. I went below deck to look for some bandages. I soon found some and tied up my shoulder.

When I was back on deck, I noticed that the ship had stopped moving and was leaning to one side. I had been too busy fighting Hands to drop the anchor. The ship had continued towards the beach until there was nowhere to go. I climbed over the side of the ship and into the shallow water below. Then I walked up to the beach and headed for the log house.

I felt proud of myself. I had saved the *Hispaniola* from the pirates and I wanted to tell my friends all about it.

CHAPTER 8

A trap

I approached the log house as quietly as I could. I crawled on my hands and knees so no one would see me. I didn't want anyone to think I was one of the pirates. If they did, they would shoot me.

I was close enough to the log house to hear my friends snoring inside. They must be sleeping peacefully. But no one was guarding them or the house. That was very strange. Why was no one on guard duty?

I was at the door now. I decided to go in and lie down in my usual place. Then they would see me in the morning. I crept through the door. Inside there was no light at all. I could see nothing in the darkness.

Suddenly, a harsh voice screamed out and I nearly jumped out of my skin.

'Pieces of eight. Pieces of eight,' screeched the voice.

It was Captain Flint, Silver's parrot. He was a better guard than any man. But what was Captain Flint doing in the log house? Had he left Silver?

On hearing the parrot, the sleeping men woke and jumped to their feet. Then I heard Long John Silver's voice. If he was in the log house, something was very wrong.

'Who's there?' he called.

I turned to run, but I bumped into someone. I pulled back and fell into the arms of another man. There was no escape now. I was a prisoner.

Someone lit a torch in the darkness and I saw the pirates. One had a bandage on his head. Silver appeared in the torchlight. Captain Flint, his parrot, sat on his shoulder as usual. Silver's face looked pale and his coat was dirty and torn.

'Hello, Jim,' he smiled. 'Have you come to visit us?'
He lit his pipe.

'Where are the others?' I asked.

'They are safe,' he said. 'Now you are here you will have to be on our side. You are a clever lad and I like you. I was like you when I was young. Join us and get the treasure. If you don't, you will have to die.'

At least Dr Livesey and the others were still alive. But now I would have to pretend to be on Silver's side just to stay alive. I didn't think I could do that.

'Why are you here? And where are my friends?' I asked. I tried to look brave.

'Yesterday morning, Dr Livesey came to see me. He told me that the *Hispaniola* had gone. When I looked out to sea, I saw that it was true. The men I left on the ship had tricked me. They had told me they wanted to join me, but they didn't. Instead they took the ship for themselves. Livesey wanted to make peace.

"If you will leave us alone, you can have the log house," he told me. "And I will look after your men if they are injured or sick."

I asked him how many of his men were still alive. He told me there were four, but he said that you had disappeared. No one knew if you were alive or dead.'

'And now you want me to join you?' I said. 'And why should I do that? You may have the log house, but what else do you have? Things are going very badly for you. You have lost the ship and most of your men. You haven't found the map and you won't find the treasure. And do you know why? Because of me, Jim Hawkins. As long as I am alive, I will use all my strength to stop you. I know exactly what your plans are. I found out about them long ago. I was sitting in the apple barrel when you were talking to your men. It was me who cut the ship's anchor rope and left it to drift. It was me who captured Hands. I will not join your band of pirates. Kill me if you want to.'

One of the pirates sprang towards me and pulled out his knife.

'That's enough. Leave the boy alone,' snapped Silver. 'I like him. He's more of a man than any of you.'

At this comment the pirates all walked outside. They were insulted by Silver's words and were not going to listen to any more insults. I could hear them muttering angrily about their captain.

'They're fools and cowards,' said Silver. 'But they are angry with me because things are going so badly. I'm on my own, Jim, and so are you. We must stick together.'

Silver was still trying to win me over to his side. I looked outside. I could see the pirates by the log house discussing something. One of them held a knife. I could see it shining in the moonlight. And for some reason another held a book.

When the pirates finished talking, they came back in. One man came forward and put something on the table. Silver looked at it.

'Look, they want to give me the black spot, Jim,' he said sadly.

'Where did you get the paper? Did you cut it out of Dr Livesey's book?' Silver asked the pirates.

'You've made a mess of everything, Silver,' said the pirate. 'We don't want you to be our captain any more.'

'Have you finished?' asked Silver quietly. He put his hand in his pocket and pulled out a piece of paper. He threw it on the floor. 'What do you think of that?'

It was the real treasure map. The pirates leaped on it like cats with a mouse. They passed it from one to another, crying out and laughing.

'We're going to get the treasure. Our clever Captain Silver has found the map,' they shouted.

Instantly, the pirates forgot their anger. They were all friends again and chattered happily about the buried treasure they were going to find.

At last, we lay down to sleep, but I stayed awake for a long time. I was afraid and my mind raced with thoughts. How could I escape from the pirates?

In the morning, I was woken by a voice coming from the woods.

'Silver, it's Dr Livesey,' called the voice.

I felt ashamed. I had left Dr Livesey and the others to go on an adventure of my own. I hadn't told anyone where I was going and now I was with the pirates.

Through a gap in the wall I could see Dr Livesey standing outside the door. Silver was leaning against the door talking to him. He sounded as friendly as he did when he was the ship's cook.

'Good morning, Doctor. We've got a surprise for you: a new face in the log house.'

'Is it Jim?' asked the doctor.

'It is,' replied Silver.

'I will look at your injured men now, Silver,' said the doctor calmly.

When Dr Livesey had bandaged the pirates' wounds and given them some medicine, he found Silver.

'I've bandaged the wounded and given the men medicine to make them better as I promised. Now I want to talk to Jim,' he said.

'No!' shouted one of the pirates.

'Let them talk,' said Silver. 'Remember, we have the treasure map. And soon we will have the treasure.' He turned to Dr Livesey. 'I saved the boy's life,' he told him. 'My men wanted to kill him, but I stopped them.'

Then he brought me to the doctor.

'Jim, why did you leave us?' the doctor asked.

'I wanted to help so I went to get the *Hispaniola* back. Then I came back to the log house, but I didn't know Silver had taken it over. As soon as I walked through the door, they captured me and I was almost killed by one of those wicked men. I wish I had stayed with you,' I sobbed.

'Come with me now, Jim. We can get away if we run fast. I can't leave you here with those pirates. They are wicked men,' said the doctor.

'No,' I sighed. 'It's too dangerous. But let me tell you some good news. I have got the ship back. She is down on the beach, ready to take us home.'

'The ship? You *have* done well, Jim. But how did you manage to do that?' smiled Dr Livesey.

I explained how I found Ben Gunn's boat and rowed it out to the *Hispaniola*. Then I told him how I cut the anchor rope and spent a night in the boat. Finally, I told him how I boarded the *Hispaniola*, captured Hands and returned the boat to the island.

Dr Livesey was amazed. He was very pleased with me. Then he called out to Silver, 'If you try to get the treasure, we will stop you.'

'I have to get the treasure,' he replied. 'If I don't, my men will kill me and Jim, too. You are the one who gave me the map.'

'I had a good reason for giving you the map. But I can't tell you now. Look after Jim, Silver,' ordered Dr Livesey.

And then he turned and walked away.

CHAPTER 9

The treasure hunt

Early the next morning, Silver sat down to breakfast with his men. As he ate his cooked meat and biscuits, Captain Flint the parrot pecked at the biscuit crumbs on Silver's coat and gave a loud squawk.

'We have got the treasure map,' he said to the pirates, 'but we haven't got the ship. We will have to find it as soon as we've got the treasure. Then we'll be on our way back to England.'

'What happens if we have any trouble from Livesey and his friends?' asked one of the pirates.

'Remember, we've got young Jim,' he replied. 'Livesey won't want us to hurt him.'

So that's why Silver wanted me. I was worried about two things. First I was worried about Silver. He was a pirate and I was sure he would stay on the side of the pirates. But if the pirates found out that he had talked to Dr Livesey, they would turn on him ... and me. He was playing a dangerous game. The second thing I was worried about was why had Dr Livesey given Silver the treasure map? Dr Livesey had come to the island to find the treasure so why did he give the map away to Silver? He couldn't find the treasure without it. What was Dr Livesey planning?

Later, we set off to find the treasure. All the pirates carried guns, knives and shovels. Some took meat and bread to eat as well. Silver tied a rope round my waist and dragged me along like a dog.

We stepped into the pirates' two rowing boats. They were covered in mud and there was water in them. But somehow they stayed afloat. We rowed to a beach on the other side of the island. Then we left the boats on the beach and walked towards a distant hill. Silver seemed to enjoy dragging me along by the rope. If ever I slowed down or stumbled, he dragged me up roughly.

As the hot sun beat down on our backs, we soon got tired. I was glad when we reached the top of the hill and Silver finally let us all sit down to rest. He took out his compass and looked at the map.

'We're looking for a very tall tree,' Silver said. 'The map shows that the treasure was buried next to it.'

Suddenly a voice sang out from the trees.

'Fifteen men on the dead man's chest,' it cried.

The pirates turned pale. I recognised the voice. It reminded me of a rusty lock.

'It's Captain Flint,' one man whispered.

'Yes, he's trying to frighten us and make us turn back,' whispered another.

'Captain Flint is dead,' said Silver firmly. 'He can't sing any more. Someone is playing a trick on us. I've been looking for that treasure for a long time. I'm going to get it and no one is going to stop me.'

'You're right,' said a pirate.

'I think I know that voice,' said another pirate.

'It's Ben Gunn. He's harmless. Come on, let's find this treasure,' cried Silver.

All the pirates calmed down and were keen to get moving again. We stood up and set off. Now that we were near to the treasure, the pirates walked faster than before. They were very excited and couldn't wait to get their hands on the treasure.

Silver pulled me along with the rope. He was just as excited as the other pirates. I slowed him down as much as possible. I was afraid. As soon as Silver had the treasure I was sure that he would kill me. That would be the end of the adventure. And the end of me.

Suddenly, the leading pirate gave a loud cry.

'That's the tree,' he shouted.

Everyone ran to the tree. Silver dragged me along with him on the end of the rope. I nearly fell over and Silver dragged me up roughly.

Next to the tree was a large hole in the ground. We all peered inside to see the treasure. But all there was inside was an empty chest. The treasure was gone.

No one could believe their eyes. All the pirates stood with their mouths open. They didn't understand. Why was the hole empty? Where was the treasure?

Suddenly one pirate dragged the empty chest out and jumped into the hole. He started digging with his hands. Two other pirates jumped in to help him. They wanted to see if the treasure was buried deeper in the hole. They could not understand the fact that the treasure had gone.

While the pirates were digging, Silver quietly passed me a gun.

'You may need that,' he whispered.

Inside the hole a pirate held up a single gold coin and shook it angrily.

'Is this all the treasure?' he shouted. 'You fool, Silver. You got it all wrong. You and your map. There is no treasure here.'

He climbed out of the hole and helped his two friends out. Then the pirates stood and glared at the captain.

'Let's fight him. And the boy,' he shouted. 'There are only two of them.

'One has a wooden leg and the other is only a boy. We can beat them easily,' laughed another pirate.

'Let's teach them a lesson they won't forget,' sneered a third pirate.

But just as the pirate raised his arm to strike me, three gunshots came from the trees.

Instantly the pirates ran off, leaving Silver and me standing by the hole.

'They are not so brave after all,' laughed Silver.

Two figures appeared from the wood. It was Dr Livesey and Ben Gunn. Dr Livesey was holding a smoking gun and Ben was behind him, also with a gun in his hand. I ran towards them.

'Dr Livesey,' I cried. 'I'm so glad to see you. Those pirates were going to beat me. You saved my life.'

'Come on. Catch those pirates,' cried out Dr Livesey. 'They'll take the *Hispaniola* unless we stop them.'

We all ran after the pirates – even Long John Silver. There was a short cut to the beach so we hurried down it. Soon we were sure we would reach the rowing boats before the pirates so we slowed to a walking pace. Silver was panting hard so we stopped to rest for a moment.

'Thank you, doctor, for saving young Jim's life and mine, too,' said Silver.

He wiped his face with a large, dirty handkerchief.

'I couldn't let young Jim come to any harm,' smiled the doctor.

I smiled back. I was so glad he had found us in time.

'How are you, Silver?' asked Ben.

Silver peered into Ben's face.

'Gunn? Is that you?' he asked.

'Yes, it's me,' Ben laughed. 'I've been on this island for three years. I found the treasure long before you all came here. I dug it up and carried it on my back to a cave in the north of the island. It's still hidden there,' he explained.

Dr Livesey spoke next.

'Jim, do you remember the day I left the log house and went to meet Ben?' he asked.

I nodded.

'Ben and I *did* meet,' continued the doctor, 'and he told me that he had dug up the treasure. After that meeting, I gave Silver the map. It was useless of course because the treasure had gone. While Silver was busy digging in the wrong place we would take the treasure from the cave to the ship.'

'So that's why you gave Silver the map,' I said.

We set off again and soon we reached the pirates' rowing boats.

'We'll use this one,' said Dr Livesey. 'And we'll smash the other one so the pirates can't use it.'

Together we smashed up one boat with lumps of rock. When it was just a pile of wood, we stepped into the other boat.

As we rowed around the island, Ben pointed to the nearby hillside. There was a tall figure standing by the black mouth of a cave. It was Squire Trelawney. He waved to us with his white handkerchief.

As we rowed further, we saw the *Hispaniola*. She was drifting in the open sea. The tide and the wind had pulled her off the beach where I had left her.

'It's a good thing we found her,' said Dr Livesey. 'She would have drifted away and we'd have been left without a ship.'

We boarded the *Hispaniola*, found the spare anchor and dropped it into the sea. Then we rowed to a little beach near Ben's cave. At last I was going to see the treasure.

CHAPTER 10

Treasure in a cave

Squire Trelawney met us at the mouth of the cave. He was glad to see me and shook my hand warmly.

'Welcome to Ben Gunn's cave, young Jim,' he said. 'I'm so glad to see you looking so well. Not that long ago I thought we would never see you again. We thought the pirates had got you.'

'I'm glad to see you, too, Squire Trelawney,' I replied. 'I'm sorry I went off on my own and worried you all.'

'Don't you worry, young Jim,' he replied. 'You are safe and well and that's all that matters.'

But when Silver greeted him, he was quite different.

'You're a wicked pirate, Long John Silver,' he said. 'But Dr Livesey wants to spare your life. I do not feel the same way. I think you are a dangerous man. Just remember how many men you have killed, how many lies you have told and how much money you have stolen.'

'Yes, sir,' said Silver politely, looking down at his boots.

We all went into the cave. It was a large place with a little stream running through it. The floor was sandy and soft to walk on.

We found Captain Smollett lying in front of a fire. Near him, thousands of gold coins, gold bars and jewels lay in great heaps, shining softly in the firelight. Here was the treasure we had come so far to find. Here was the treasure that had cost so many lives and caused so much suffering.

Many men had risked their lives to find it.

Had it been worth it? I wondered.

What a dinner we had together that evening. Ben Gunn cooked goat's meat for us all and we added things to it from the stores on the *Hispaniola*. Everyone was so happy that night. We had the treasure, we had the ship back and soon we would be going home.

In the morning, Dr Livesey and Squire Trelawney took the first load of treasure back to the *Hispaniola*. It was a 15-minute walk from the cave to the beach. Then it took 30 minutes to row from there to the ship. There was a lot to carry and the gold was very heavy. It took three days to load all the treasure onto the ship. We knew there were still some pirates on the island so we kept a careful lookout all the time.

My job was to sit in the cave, sort the coins and pack them into cloth bags. I enjoyed sorting the coins. There was such a strange collection. Some were English coins and some were French. Some were Spanish coins and some were Portuguese. There were a few from other places, too.

It took me two days to sort and pack the huge pile of coins. When I had filled a few bags, I carried them to the entrance of the cave. From here, Ben Gunn carried the treasure to the beach. Then Dr Livesey rowed it all to the *Hispaniola* where Squire Trelawney and Silver were waiting for him. Finally the squire and Silver unloaded the rowing boat and loaded the treasure onto the ship. Then Dr Livesey rowed back to the beach and waited for Ben Gunn to appear with the next load of treasure.

On the third day, when we had finally finished loading the treasure onto the *Hispaniola*, I stood near the cave with Dr Livesey and Silver. All of a sudden we heard men shouting and screaming.

'It's the pirates,' I cried. 'They're coming to find us. And the treasure.'

Dr Livesey shook his head.

'I don't think we're in any danger, Jim,' he said. 'They sound as if they are sick. I am a doctor and if they need my help, I will go to them.'

'Don't do that, Dr Livesey,' replied Silver. 'They are cowards, but they are cruel men. It's a trick. They want you to think they are weak. They want you to go to them. Then they will kill you.'

'Very well,' replied Dr Livesey. 'But I think we should leave some goat's meat and biscuits for them in the cave. We can leave some medicine for them, too.'

So we placed these things in the cave, together with some tools, some rope and some clothes. Dr Livesey left some bullets so that they could shoot animals for food.

When all the treasure was on board the *Hispaniola*, we took some water and goat meat for the journey.

Captain Smollett said, 'There's just one more thing we must do. The *Hispaniola* must fly the Union Flag.'

We hung the Union Flag on the flagpole. And then, on that fine sunny morning, we pulled up the anchor. At last we were on our way home.

As we passed the south point of the island, we saw the pirates on the beach. They were kneeling in the sand and holding out their hands, begging us not to leave them behind on the island.

'What should we do?' I asked. 'Should we take them with us or should we leave them on the island?'

Squire Trelawney frowned.

'If we took them back to England, they would be put in prison,' he said. 'It would be kinder to leave them here on the island.'

Dr Livesey called out to them.

'We can't take you back with us,' he shouted. 'But we've left you some food and medicine. There are tools, rope and clothes, too. We left them over there for you.' He pointed towards the cave. 'In that cave.'

When we passed close by the pirates, one of them gave a loud cry of rage and fired his gun at us. The bullet whizzed past Silver's head. He quickly ducked down and it just missed him. That was the last we saw of them. It was the last we saw of Treasure Island, too.

Soon we were far out at sea. Sailing the ship was hard work because the weather was stormy and we didn't have enough men.

Captain Smollett was a little better, but he still needed to rest. He lay on a mattress on the deck and called out his orders to the rest of us.

It was clear that we would have to find more sailors so Captain Smollett told us to head for the nearest port. This was in South America. It was a long way away and we had to sail for several hours. By sunset, the port finally came into sight.

'Land ahoy!' shouted the captain from his mattress.

Everyone was very tired from all the hard work and glad to see dry land again.

When the ship was safely tied to the dock, Dr Livesey, Squire Trelawney and I went ashore. What a welcoming sight it was. The port was full of suntanned men wandering around selling many different types of fruit and vegetables. We smiled when we saw their friendly faces under the twinkling lights.

As we walked around the little town, we met an English sea captain. He was a friendly man and invited us to go on board his ship. We happily agreed. The sea captain gave us a good meal. We told each other tales of our adventures and as the time passed by, the stories became more and more exciting.

When we finally got back to the *Hispaniola*, the sun was coming up. We had been much longer than we planned to be. We found Benn Gunn alone on deck. He looked very upset and he had very bad news to tell us: Silver had gone. And he had taken a big bag of treasure with him. Long John Silver had shown us that he *was* a pirate and like all pirates he would steal if he got the chance. He had seen the chance, taken it and got clean away.

'The wicked thief. He will be caught and punished,' growled Squire Trelawney. 'I wish I could do it myself.'

But there was nothing we could do. We hired our new crew and took on more food and water. Then we set off for home.

It was a long journey, but we had no more adventures. When at last we sailed into Bristol, I was happy to be back in my own country. At last I would see my mother again.

As we unloaded the ship, Dr Livesey said, 'Of the men who started this adventure, only four are left: Squire Trelawney, Captain Smollett, Jim and me.'

Each of us had a share of the treasure. Squire Trelawney went back to the Hall and Dr Livesey became a doctor again. Captain Smollett decided not to go back to sea. Ben Gunn had a share of the treasure, too, but he spent it all in three weeks. He was soon looking for another ship to sail on.

We heard no more of Long John Silver, the one-legged pirate. I hope that journey was his last. I hope he was caught as pirates usually are and punished for his life as a pirate captain.

As for me, Jim Hawkins, I shall never forget my great adventure. In my dreams I still see the wild shores of Treasure Island. I still hear Captain Flint the parrot squawking, 'Pieces of eight. Pieces of eight.'

But I am happy enough now. After my journey to Treasure Island, I promised myself that I would never go to sea again. And I never did.

Ocean Travel

If I could travel
the oceans blue,
these are the things
that I would do:

Fly with puffins
under the sea.
Dive with seagulls.
Fish for my tea.

Cling to the tail
of a rolling whale.
Leap with dolphins
in a buffeting gale.

Soar with an eagle.
Hunt with a shark.
Frolic with seals.
Fly home before dark.

Jennifer Tweedie

A pirate ship

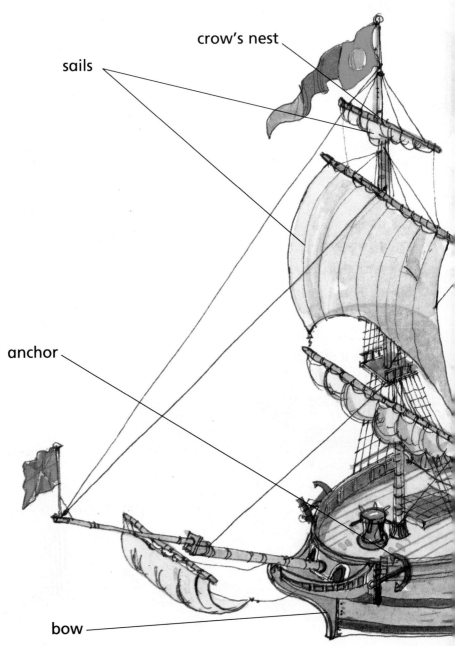

crow's nest

sails

anchor

bow

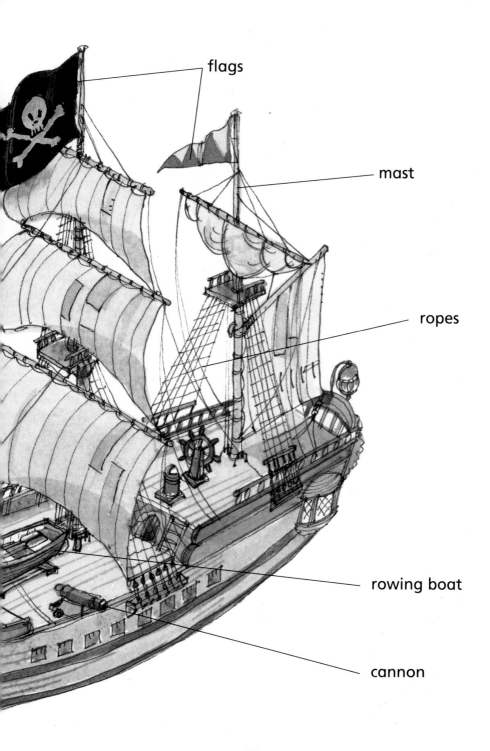

flags

mast

ropes

rowing boat

cannon

About the author – Robert Louis Stevenson

 Robert Louis Stevenson was born in Edinburgh, Scotland, in 1850. His father was an engineer and his family wanted Robert to be one, too. But he decided to go to Edinburgh University to study law instead.

In his early 20s he became ill with a chest problem. He suffered from this for the rest of his life. He moved from place to place, trying to find a suitable climate. He decided that he wanted to be a writer, not a lawyer.

In 1880 Robert married an American woman called Fanny Osbourne in California, USA. She already had two children.

In 1890 Robert and his family finally settled on an island called Upolu in Samoa. He built a big house which he called Vailima (Five Rivers). The Samoan people loved him and called him Tusitala (teller of tales).

Robert Louis Stevenson died of a stroke in 1894. He was buried at the top of a mountain.